D0573822

ESPN HOST **MIKE GREENBERG** &
STACY STEPONATE GREENBERG

MVP

Most Valuable Puppy

Illustrated by
Bonnie Pang

ALADDIN   NEW YORK   LONDON   TORONTO   SYDNEY   NEW DELHI

For Nikki and Stephen, who bring laughter and joy to our lives every single day
—Mom and Dad

For my parents, who encouraged me to doodle on paper napkins
—B. P.

ALADDIN An imprint of Simon & Schuster Children's Publishing Division | 1230 Avenue of the Americas, New York, New York 10020 | First Aladdin hardcover edition June 2018 | Copyright © 2018 by Mike and Stacy Greenberg | Illustrations by Bonnie Pang | All rights reserved, including the right of reproduction in whole or in part in any form. | ALADDIN and related logo are registered trademarks of Simon & Schuster, Inc. For information about special discounts for bulk purchases, please contact Simon & Schuster Special Sales at 1-866-506-1949 or business@simonandschuster.com. | The Simon & Schuster Speakers Bureau can bring authors to your live event. For more information or to book an event contact the Simon & Schuster Speakers Bureau at 1-866-248-3049 or visit our website at www.simonspeakers.com. | Designed by Karin Paprocki and Tiara Iandiorio | The illustrations for this book were rendered digitally. The text of this book was set in Candy Square BTN. Manufactured in China 0318 SCP | 10 9 8 7 6 5 4 3 2 1 This book has been cataloged with the Library of Congress. | ISBN 978-1-4814-8931-7 (hc) ISBN 978-1-4814-8932-4 (eBook)

Hi! My name is Phoebe! I like tummy scratches, chasing tennis balls, and eating crumbs that fall from the kitchen table.

More than anything, though, I love my family. The day I met them was the very best day of my entire life.

My sister, The Girl with the Curly Hair, walked right over to me. Our eyes met. We both smiled. When she scratched my tummy, my pink tail started swishing so fast. We were best friends at first sight.

So now I live with my family, and every day is a new adventure. Each morning starts with me watching Dad, The Man with the Beard, talking about sports in his box.

I'm pretty sure I could be very good at sports!

That's my brother, The Baby, over there.
He's really the boss around here. Every time
he makes a sound, Mom, The Lady Who
Feeds Me, rushes to his side.

My brother rolls from his tummy to his back. I could do that a million times! But when my brother does it, Mom cheers and takes pictures.

When my brother starts walking and talking, running and jumping, he can play with my sister and me.

My favorite time of day is when my sister comes home from school. I wait for her, and when she gets off the bus, she always throws a ball for me to catch.

Then it's snack time! I like to lick the crumbs from her fingers, and when I roll over, she gives me a treat.

Next it's playground time!

There are some kids playing soccer nearby.

I have learned all about soccer from watching The Man with the Beard in his box, so I join right in.

I score a goal,

dive for a save,

steal the ball,

lick a goalie,

and all the while see my sister laughing and cheering.

Can you play football, too?

I run straight to my sister and pick up the football. Our eyes meet. We both smile.

I guess you could say we both know she is ready to give it a try.

Then, just as she is about to score
a touchdown . . .

she trips, falls flat on her face, and drops the ball. It just slips out of her hands.

The Girl with the Curly Hair looks like she might cry. I know what I have to do. It is time for me to save the day.

I run forward and back. I score a
touchdown for one team . . .

and then for the other.

All the boys and girls are chasing
me and laughing, except my sister.
She is still sitting where she fell,
looking sad.

She smiles and calls my name. I run straight toward her, and just as I am about to jump into her lap . . . a squirrel runs by. Did I forget to mention I love chasing squirrels?

SQUIRREL!

When the squirrel runs up a tree, the kids and I fall to the ground, tired from running so fast and laughing so hard.